World of Reading

LEVEL 1

THIS IS ANT-MAN

Adapted by Chris "Doc" Wyatt

Illustrated by Ron Lim *and* Rachelle Rosenberg

Based on the Marvel comic book character Ant-Man

ABDO
Spotlight

Los Angeles
New York

ABDOPUBLISHING.COM

Reinforced library bound edition published in 2018 by Spotlight, a division of ABDO, PO Box 398166, Minneapolis, Minnesota 55439. Spotlight produces high-quality reinforced library bound editions for schools and libraries. Published by Marvel Press, an imprint of Disney Book Group.

Printed in the United States of America, North Mankato, Minnesota.
042017
092017

MARVEL
marvelkids.com

THIS BOOK CONTAINS
RECYCLED MATERIALS

© 2015 MARVEL

LIBRARY OF CONGRESS CATALOGING-IN-PUBLICATION DATA

This title was previously cataloged with the following information:

Wyatt, Chris.
 This is Ant-Man / adapted by Chris "Doc" Wyatt ; illustrated by Ron Lim and Rachelle Rosenberg ; based on the Marvel comic book character Ant-Man.
   p. cm. -- (World of reading. Level 1)
 Summary: Introduces Scott Lang and discusses how he became the hero known as Ant-Man.
 1. Superheroes--Juvenile fiction. 2. Adventure stories. 3. Superheroes--Fiction. 4. Adventure and adventurers--Fiction. 5. Adventure stories. 6. Superheroes. I. Lim, Ron and Rosenberg, Rachelle, ill.
 PZ7.W96598 Th 2015
 [E]--dc23

                2014944510

978-1-5321-4048-8 (Reinforced Library Bound Edition)

Spotlight
A Division of ABDO
abdopublishing.com

This is Scott Lang.

Scott is Ant-Man.

Ant-Man is a Super Hero!

Scott was not always Ant-Man.
He was once a thief.

Scott stole to support his family.

Scott wanted to teach his daughter
right from wrong.
He decided to stop stealing.
He went back to school to study science.

One day, Scott met a scientist
named Hank.
They talked about science.

Hank gave Scott a special suit.
Scott tried it on.

Scott shrank to the size of an ant!
It was fun at first.

But then ants chased Scott!

Scott got big again
and saved himself!

Soon Scott found a way
to talk to ants.

Then they were his friends.

Scott became Ant-Man.

Ant-Man fights Super Villains.

Ant-Man uses the ants as an army.

Now Ant-Man helps the Avengers.

Being small helps Ant-Man
do special things.

Bad guys cannot see him coming.

Ant-Man can fit in small places.

Ant-Man can surprise bad guys!

Ant-Man likes working with Iron Man.

Ant-Man and Iron Man
make a good team.

Ant-Man is very strong!

Ant-Man can turn from big to tiny.

Ant-Man fights for good.

Ant-Man has lots of
Super Hero friends.

They help each other
fight the bad guys!

Ant-Man is a true hero.